Dear Father Christmas

For Eva – J.W.

For Yumi – R.R.

PUFFIN BOOKS

Published by the Penguin Group: London, New York, Australia,
Canada, India, Ireland, New Zealand and South Africa
Penguin Books Ltd, Registered Offices:
80 Strand, London WC2R 0RL, England

puffinbooks.com

First published in Puffin Books 2008
1 3 5 7 9 10 8 6 4 2
Text copyright © Jeanne Willis, 2008
Illustrations copyright © Rosie Reeve, 2008
All rights reserved
The moral right of the author and illustrator has been asserted
Made and printed in China
ISBN: 978-0-141-50209-0

Dear Father Christmas

Jeanne Willis

Rosie Reeve

PUFFIN

Dear Father Christmas,
I've been very,

very

good . . .

I'm writing you this letter
Because Mummy said I should.

I know I mustn't ask for much,
But this is what I'd like –

No more fluffy
slippers, thanks,

I do not need a bike.

I'm very fond of teddies
But I think I've got enough.

I've got an awful lot of toys
And games and books and stuff.

But if you really love me
May I have a special spray

That keeps the scary monsters
And the big bad wolf away?

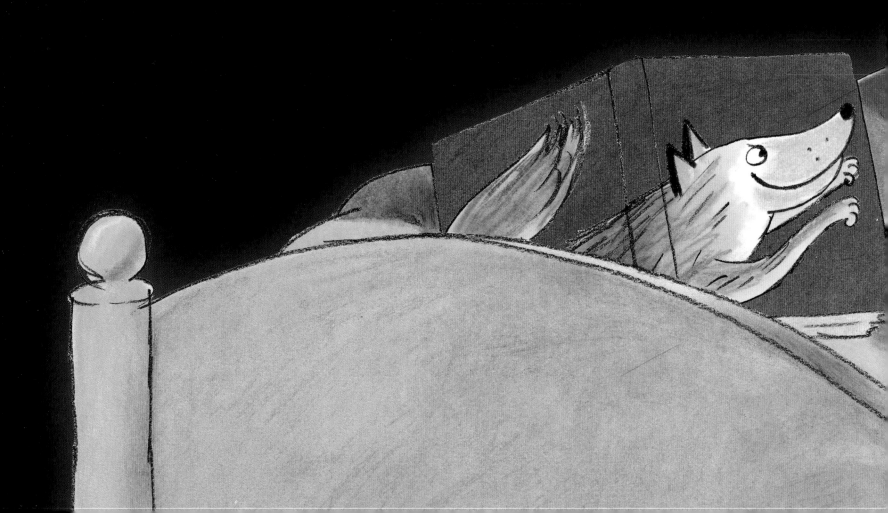

And could I have some laces

That can do up by themselves?

A ladder that can reach the sweets
That sit on too-high shelves?

And dear Father Christmas
If you're really, really clever,

May I have a little hamster
Who will always live forever?

And on the days
when I'm at school

And fall and hurt
my knee,

Could you fix it so that Mum
Can come and cuddle me?

And may I have a magic wand
That brings some special snow

To make my snowman come to life?
I'd love him to, you know.

And please could you ask Grandma
If she'd like to come and stay

And live with us for always?
It would make my Christmas Day.

And when I hang my stocking up
Just leave a small gift there –

A little baby brother
With big eyes and curly hair.

Dear Father Christmas,
I hope you read my list.

I cannot think of anything
Important that I've missed.

Except my greatest Christmas wish,
I hope it will come true –

When you fly your sleigh tonight . . .

Dad, please can I come too . . . ?

Lots
of
love,
Mary Christmas
x X x

❄ Why not write your own letter to Father Christmas?

❄ First, tear out the sheet opposite
and write down your Christmas wish.
(Don't forget to write your address at the top.)

❄ Use some of the stickers to decorate the page, if you like.

❄ Then fold along the dotted lines, so that Father Christmas's
address is on the outside, and seal with a sticker.

❄ You could even draw a picture on the envelope,
or decorate it with more stickers!

❄ Last of all, pop it in a post box . . .

I live at . . .

Dear Father Christmas,

Love from,

Father Christmas
North Pole
SAN TA1